NIGHTLITEPUBLISHING.COM

~ DEDICATION ~

Special thanks to my three daughters,

Amber, Autumn and Ayana...

who have never wavered in their support for me and all of my endeavors.

Special, special thanks to Autumn who helped so much to bring this project to fruition.

--- P.C.H.

Akilah loved her big black teddy bear

She loved her swing an awful lot

She loved her puppy, Mo Mo Dear

She loved the shoes that she just got

But what she really loved much more
was Mommy, Daddy and sister Zora

She loved to play with Teddy Bear

Swing on her swing with puppy near

Her bright red shoes made her feet dance fast

But then she felt a little sad because
the fun would never last

She couldn't play with her mommy

She was always in the kitchen cooking

She couldn't play with her daddy
He was always sad and tired-looking

She couldn't play with sister Zora

She was always on the phone with Nora

What could she do to make fun last
and not leave her heart so very fast?

She went into the kitchen and asked her mommy, "Can I help you cook something yummy?"

"Of course my dear, oh my, oh my, oh my I could use some help with this sweet potato pie."

And then her mommy smiled

Her daddy was lying on the couch "Can
I get you a pillow-the one that's red?"

"Thank you, Sweetheart
I could use a pillow for my aching head"

And then her daddy smiled

Zora was sitting in her room
talking loudly on the phone
"Can I match your socks and put
them away?"

"Why thank you, Akilah
That would just make my day"

And then her sister smiled

Akilah went to bed that night
In hopes of having sweet, sweet dreams
She closed her eyes and held them tight

And saw a palace fit for kings
And then for miles and miles and miles
High, way high up to the stars
Were beautiful, endless, humongous smiles
They were so high they reached to Mars.

Happy deeds and acts of love
She would give her family piles and piles
And her heart would be the home of
The eternal kingdom of happy smiles.

www.ingramcontent.com/pod-product-compliance
Lightning Source LLC
Chambersburg PA
CBHW041010170626
46815CB00002B/237